DAN FREEDMAN

Published by I_AM Self-Publishing, 2016

ISBN 978-1-911079-25-5

PRAISE FOR THE JAMIE JOHNSON SERIES

"You'll read this and want to get out there and play"
Steven Gerrard

"An inspiring read for all football fans"
Gary Lineker

"If you like football, this book's for you"
Frank Lampard

"Jamie could go all the way"
Jermain Defoe

"I love reading about football and it doesn't get much better than this"
Joe Hart

"Pure joy"
The Times

"Inspiring"
Observer

"Gripping"
Sunday Express

"A resounding victory"
Telegraph

About the Author

Dan Freedman grew up wanting to be a professional footballer. That didn't happen. But he went on to become a top football journalist, personally interviewing the likes of Cristiano Ronaldo, Lionel Messi, David Beckham and Sir Alex Ferguson.

He uses his passion and knowledge of football to write the hugely popular series of Jamie Johnson football novels. When he is not writing, Dan delivers talks and workshops for schools. And he still plays football whenever he can.

www.DanFreedman.co.uk

Follow Dan on Twitter
@DanFreedman99

Acknowledgements

Thanks to:

Mum, Ivan, Dad, Linda, Liz and Sam for all your support. Special extra thanks to Brian – great to work with you.

William Major Bolitho for your fantastic ideas.

Vicky Toubian, Tina Grant, Susie Rickard, Stuart Mawhinney, Adam Bernard, Rowena Simmons, Xabi de Beristain Humphrey, Ena McNamara, Tim Gentles, Struan Marshall, Martin Hitchcock, Henry Winter, Paul Hayward, Glenn Moore, Matt Dickinson, Phillip Howard Glyn, Jonathan Kaye, Jim Sells, Elliott Moore, Claire Lewis, Matt Kleinman and Phil Abbott for your support and expert advice.

The Youth Sport Trust for letting me be part of your work.

Hazel Ruscoe – this story is inspired by ideas we had together.

Sam and Joe Talbot, Sue Nott, Amy Buscombe, Shaun Duggan, Sally Rosser, Carlene Marshall-King, the exceptional cast led by Louis Dunn and all at Short Form Film and the BBC for bringing Jamie to life on the screen.

Lola Cashman for keeping me going all those years ago when I wanted to give up.

The brilliant Ali Dewji, Leila Dewji, Sarah Stewart and Jason Cox for putting this book into people's hands.

And to you for reading Jamie's story.

JAMIE JOHNSON

DAN FREEDMAN

1

Over His Head

Thursday 14 October

The ball was in the air.

Jamie had his back to the goal.

He knew he had to try it.

If he pulled it off, if he scored with an overhead kick in front of everyone in the playground, Jamie Johnson knew it would be one of the best moments of his life.

It would shut up Bryn Staunton and Tyler Forbes for days and it would prove, once and for all, that he was easily the best player in the whole of Year Seven.

Although he had all the other skills, Jamie had never done a proper overhead kick before – but he knew he had to go for it. Now.

Jamie kept his eye on the ball, as it seemed to hover above his shoulder. Then he launched his body into the air to meet it.

Jamie flew high above the hard cement of the playground, his body soaring towards its target.

In the air, he snapped his legs back over his head in a scissor-like motion, just as he'd seen the best players do on TV.

He closed his eyes and waited for the contact with the ball. He wanted to hammer it home. He waited and hoped for the sweet sensation of the perfect strike.

But it didn't come. He felt his left foot barely scuff the side of the ball, slicing it sideways. And now, gravity played its part, dragging Jamie back down to earth with alarming speed.

Jamie crashed back down onto the gravel with a loud, wet, painful thud.

His mind screamed with anger, while his body stung with the pain. The entire layer of skin on Jamie's kneecap had been scraped off.

The blood from his gravel-filled knee started to spill through the hole in his trousers.

Jamie Johnson was going to be a big star one day. He just knew it. He wanted to be a professional footballer when he grew up. And not just any old professional footballer. He wanted to be the best. He wanted everyone in the world to know who Jamie Johnson was. And sometimes, if he closed his eyes and concentrated hard enough, he could already imagine the fans singing his name:

One Jamie Johnson... There's only one Jamie Johnson...

But that was not the song that the other boys were singing in the playground today.

Instead, as Jamie wiped his dirty, wet hands down his bloodied trousers, Bryn Staunton and Tyler Forbes were singing:

"He's small, he's thick, he can't do overhead kicks! He's Jamie Johnson, Jamie Johnson..."

This was easily the second most embarrassing moment of Jamie's life. The only time that beat it was the day when, at his primary school, Wheatlands, he had wet himself at the end of assembly – in front of the whole school. That was horrendous, but this wasn't far behind. Jamie didn't mind looking like a fool in lessons, or people taking the mickey out of him for wearing old clothes, but he never thought the day would come where people would tease him about how he played football.

He wanted people to think of him as a football genius. But right now, he looked like a football chump.

These matches at break-time were the most important part of the day for all the footballers at school. If you were on the winning side, you were king for the rest of the day. If you lost, you knew you wouldn't be allowed to forget it.

Bryn Staunton and Tyler Forbes – the two biggest boys in Jamie's year – always made sure that they were on the same side in break, and they never picked Jamie. Ever.

It wasn't because he wasn't good enough; in fact, it was the exact opposite. It was *because* Jamie was the best player in the whole year that they had it in for him.

"Forget about them," said Hugo Bogson, the only real friend that Jamie had made at The Grove so far, helping Jamie up. "They're idiots."

"Thanks," said Jamie, carefully avoiding Hugo's outstretched hand, which was filthy.

They were mates and Jamie appreciated Hugo sticking up for him, but he also knew that Hugo was one of the dirtiest people he'd ever met. Jamie always tried not to touch him directly.

Still, no matter how weird Hugo Bogson was, he wasn't ever horrible to other kids in the way that Bryn and Tyler were. In fact, Jamie had never seen Hugo be mean to anyone, and that's what Jamie liked about him.

2

Wish List

It took Jamie ages to get home from school. He missed the bus and had to stand waiting in the rain for 20 minutes for the next one to come. He was drenched to the bone by the time he got in.

Some of the other kids called their mums and got lifts home, but Jamie couldn't do that. His mum was on a late shift at the hospital. She wouldn't be home until 10. And anyway, even if she was home, she couldn't have given him a lift. Her car was broken. It had just been sitting uselessly in the drive for the last six months and now it was going to cost way too much to fix.

Sometimes, Jamie felt sorry for his mum. It was a horrible feeling to have. He knew you shouldn't feel sorry for your parents.

Jamie wondered how he would feel if his mum got married again. Loads of the kids at school hated their stepdads. But Jamie wouldn't mind. He just wanted his mum to be happy. If she wanted to get married again, that would be fine by Jamie – as long as the bloke was a Hawkstone United fan! That would be his only demand!

Jamie put the chicken and noodles his mum had left him into the microwave and turned it on to full power. Then he checked the time: 8.18p.m. His granddad, Mike, would be over soon to check he was OK. He always did that when Jamie's mum was working. It was cool; they just watched TV together and Mike let Jamie watch whatever he wanted!

In a way, it was good that Jamie's mum wasn't home. If she had been, Jamie would have had to explain the state his trousers were in and then his mum would have got angry about buying a new pair.

"We're not exactly rolling in it, Jamie!" he could imagine her saying.

While his dinner was cooking, Jamie ripped a piece of paper from the pad next to the phone and sat down on a stool in the kitchen. He began to write down his wish list of things that he wanted to happen in his life:

JAMIE JOHNSON - 10 THNGS I WANT

Written on Oct 14 - ageD 11 and 1/2 (nearly)

1. To do PROPER overhead kicks
2. To be rich when I'm older
3. New shinpads (mine are finished, every kick kills my shins!)
4. A younger brother so I can teach him football and other stuff
5. To buy a new car for mum

~~6. Kiss J~~

6. To learn Tae Kwon Do off jack so no one messes with me!!
7. Have big muscles (including a 6 pack!)
8. To be REALLY famous so everyone knows me
9. TO BE A PROFESSIONAL FOOTBALLER!

The ping of the microwave went before Jamie had written down number 10.

He'd fill that one in another time. Plus, if he could achieve number nine then nothing else would matter anyway!

If he became a professional footballer, Jamie Johnson could have everything he wanted.

That night, as he got into bed and turned out his light, Jamie's mood darkened. He'd had a good evening with Mike but now, just as he wanted to get to sleep, he began to feel unsettled. His thoughts and worries were swimming like evil sharks around his mind.

He tried to fend them off by focusing on good things, like football. He asked himself questions: how much money would his favourite team, Hawkstone United, spend in the next transfer window? What would his top world 11 be?

Normally, football kept the bad feelings away. But tonight, it was no good. The negative thoughts were taking over his brain...

Why did his life have to be so hard? Why couldn't he have a nice, easy life like the other kids?

Two parents and a car that worked – was that too much to ask for?!

Jamie didn't want to go to school the next day. He didn't want to be the butt of any more jokes. He didn't even want to be Jamie Johnson any more.

Maybe he should give up playing football and do sprinting instead. The athletics coach at school had said that he was quick enough to be a professional sprinter; that if he trained hard, he could go to the Olympics... But athletics wasn't Jamies sport. He loved football. He always would. And Bryn and Tyler were trying to stop Jamie doing what he loved most.

The wind was tapping angrily at Jamie's window now. Jamie could almost hear it whistling, taunting him, just like the others had done in the playground:

He's short, he's sad, he doesn't have a dad...
He's Jamie Johnson, Jamie Johnson...

As he pulled the duvet tight around himself, Jamie felt the sting of a tear prick the corner of his eye.

But, as he wiped it away, a surge of determination sprang up inside him.

He knew exactly why Bryn and Tyler targeted him: Jamie played left wing in The Grove's school team and left wing was Tyler Forbes' position too. So, as long as Jamie was playing, Tyler couldn't get in the team. He and Bryn, being best mates, had made a plan to try to get Jamie out... to try to stop him playing football altogether.

Jamie's granddad, Mike, had warned him this would happen; that he would always be a target for people who weren't as good as him.

They were jealous of his talent. They were jealous because they wished they could do the things with a football that Jamie could do.

"Never give up," Mike had always told him. "Just keep coming back for more. And if someone ever tries to make you feel small, you stand up for yourself!"

Jamie turned over and clenched his fists into his chest.

Bryn and Tyler wanted to stop Jamie doing what he did best. They wanted to stop him playing. But Jamie wouldn't let them. No one would ever stop him playing football.

It was time for Jamie to stand up for himself.

3

The Sandwich

Friday 15 October

When the bell went and everyone went outside for break, Jamie decided to stay in the classroom for a bit. Hugo was staying inside too. Maybe Jamie would see what Hugo was doing at the weekend.

It wasn't as if Jamie didn't have other mates outside school – of course he did. For a start, he had Jack – the best mate in the world. She and Jamie had been best friends all the way through primary school and Jamie only really felt like himself when he was chilling with her.

But at The Grove, Jamie pretty much just had Hugo.

He and Hugo had kind of just been thrown together. They lived quite near each other and, by the end of the first week at The Grove, they were the only two who didn't belong to any of the gangs. So they decided to form their own gang. Of two.

They didn't exactly make a scary pair, but at least it meant they both had someone to go around with, and they always sat next to each other at lunch.

Not that they had a whole lot in common.

Jamie was quite shy, especially with people he didn't know that well, and Hugo ... well, there was no other way to say it... Hugo was a little weird.

He took delight in the strangest things. Bogies were a particular delicacy for him, whether they were his or someone else's!

But, above all else, Hugo's number-one speciality was farting. He could do all sorts: silent, potent, eggy ... but he was a real expert at the loud ones. His best ones sounded like a duck quacking!

He was so proud of each fart he did that he wanted to tell the whole world about them.

"Can you smell it yet?" he'd ask Jamie when he'd let rip, his eyes gleaming with excitement.

If Jamie had a pound for every time that Hugo had asked him to "pull his finger", Jamie would already be a millionaire!

Jamie stared as Hugo carefully unwrapped his sandwiches. Jamie felt like a scientist studying a wild monkey.

As soon as the sandwiches came out of the silver foil, the smell immediately invaded Jamie's nostrils.

They smelled like poo! They reeked so badly, Jamie thought that he was going to heave. Then he saw that brown, jellied juices were beginning to drip down the side of the bread...

"Man! What's in that sandwich?" Jamie yelled, covering his nose as Hugo tucked in. "It looks like dog food!"

Hugo Bogson just stared back at Jamie. He didn't say anything. Instead he just smiled, and then he took another big bite of his sandwich.

"I'm sorry, Hugo, but that's rank!" laughed Jamie. "I'm going to play football!"

And with that, Jamie practically sprinted out of the room.

It was a cold, wet day and the air from Jamie's mouth immediately froze into white clouds in front of him. They were so thick it looked as if Jamie was breathing out smoke.

Jamie thrust his hands into his pockets to keep them warm. Most of the other kids were wearing gloves. But Jamie didn't like wearing them. They made his hands feel trapped.

The match had already started and the players on either side were running about after the ball like madmen. None of them were holding their positions. They just all swarmed around after the ball.

In the middle of the playground, someone had been sick and the caretaker had put a load of sawdust over the top of it to soak up the liquid.

"What's the score?" Jamie asked, standing on the side of the playground. "Which side shall I go on?"

He wished that someone would just ask him to be on their side. He wished that for once he could be part of a gang at The Grove. Not always an outsider. If his mum had listened to him and sent him to Kingfield with Jack then he wouldn't have any of these stupid problems.

"Who said you can play anyway?" shouted Bryn, coming across to confront Jamie.

"Free country!" Jamie shouted back. "Who made you king?"

"Right," shouted Bryn, "let's get him!"

Suddenly Bryn and Tyler sprinted over to the heap of wet sawdust. Then they grabbed some of it in their gloves!

And now they were running towards Jamie with balls of sawdust and sick pressed in the palms of their gloves, ready to release. It was as if they'd invented a new game called sickball! Except Jamie didn't have any weapons of his own.

But he had something else. His pace.

Jamie immediately hit top speed, twisting and swerving in different directions to avoid his pursuers.

Bryn and Tyler knew there was no way they would be able to catch Jamie in a straight race, but they had two against one, so they split into different directions to make sure that they could trap him.

Soon they were coming at Jamie from either side. He was cornered. He had to stop.

"OK, guys," he said, putting his hands up. "You got me. But you don't have to do this, you know."

"Course we don't have to do it, you idiot!" Tyler sniggered, looking at the disgusting parcel of sick and sawdust in his glove. "We *want* to do it!"

"Guys, really... trust me, you don't," said Jamie, looking to his left and his right as an idea suddenly came into his head. It was such a good idea that he couldn't help but start smiling.

"What are you laughing at?" shouted Bryn angrily. "This'll shut you up!"

And simultaneously, he and Tyler Forbes launched their sick missiles at him.

Jamie had half a millisecond in which to work, if he was to get his plan right. As soon as he saw the rockets heading towards him, he ducked as quickly as he could. He could feel the breeze of the sickballs whoosh over the top of his head.

The rockets just missed him, and each other, as they crossed paths in the air. Instead, they carried on their journeys. By the time Bryn and Tyler actually realized what was happening, it was too late! Their own sickballs were heading straight for them, and there was no time for them to get out of the way!

SPLAT!!

The sickballs smashed into their faces and oozed down the side of their cheeks. Some went in Bryn's hair and it looked as if some had even gone into Tyler's mouth.

While they were still in shock, spitting sawdust out of their mouths and wiping sick off their faces, Jamie stood up and pointed at them.

"Who's stupid now?" he laughed. "Serves you right!"

Then he started running back to the school building. It was almost time for lessons.

He knew they'd chase after him.

But he also knew they'd never catch him. Not today, anyway...

4

Glory Days

Saturday 16 October

"And none of your secret fish and chip dinners on the way home, Dad!" Jamie's mum shouted to her dad, Mike, as he and Jamie headed off to the Hawkstone game. "I know what you two get up to!"

"OK, love," replied Mike, full of sincerity.

But as they left the house, he gave Jamie a wink and a smile.

"What she doesn't know won't hurt her!" they said in unison, as soon as they were out of earshot.

Jamie absolutely loved going to Hawkstone games with Mike. They didn't have enough money to get a season ticket, but in a way, that meant that the games they did get to go to were even more special.

Football had linked Mike and Jamie pretty much since the day Jamie was born.

Mike had bought Jamie his first football when he was three years old. It was the best present that Jamie had ever had.

For Jamie, what set Mike apart from everyone else, what made him so cool was that he had once been a professional footballer for Hawkstone. Jamie thought that, since Mike had done it, maybe there was a chance he could do it too.

As they walked the three-kilometre journey to the ground and joined the hordes of other fans making the same pilgrimage, Jamie felt really mature. Almost like an adult.

When Jamie was younger, Mike used to carry him all the way to the ground on his shoulders. He was a really strong man and Jamie loved that feeling of being so high in the air, looking down on everyone else. And the funny thing was that, even now, when he was with Mike, Jamie still felt six feet tall.

"Here it is," said Mike. "Here's that photo I was telling you about."

Mike had stopped by one of the large photos next to the catering area inside the ground.

Jamie looked at the photo and the plaque underneath it, which read:

VICTORIOUS HAWKS
UNITED'S FIRST-EVER YOUTH CUP
WINNING TEAM

"This was the day we won the Youth Cup," Mike said, shaking his head wistfully. "I can't believe that was 40 years ago... I look about as old as you look now!"

"Which one's you, Mike?" said Jamie, searching the faces of the players for one who looked like a younger version of his granddad.

"That's me," said Mike, pointing to a big tank of a player in the back row. "Those were my glory days, JJ."

Jamie looked at the photo. His eyes zoomed in to the picture of his grandfather as a young man. He looked so strong, so healthy... so happy.

Jamie wanted to be just like Mike and maybe, one day, as good as him.

"Shall I tell you what the trick of life is, Jamie?" said Mike, putting his hand on his grandson's shoulder. "Realizing that sometimes you only get one shot at something. So when that chance comes along, you'd sure as hell better take it."

5
Warm-Up

Jamie and Mike always liked to get to their seats in time for the warm-up because it meant they got to see a different side to the players than the one they saw during the game.

They caught a glimpse of the players' *real* characters – those who liked a laugh and those who were deadly serious. They could see who the good mates were by the way they paired off to do their stretches … and they could also see who had the most skills, as the warm-up was a chance to show off!

There was no doubt that Hawkstone's most skilful player was their young midfielder, Glenn Richardson.

His passing vision was unbelievable. Jamie reckoned he could have even played the game blindfolded and still known exactly where all his teammates were on the pitch.

But Hawkstone's most important, inspirational player was the captain, Harry Armstrong. He was Jamie's favourite-ever player and Jamie was watching him now, as he went around each member of his team, geeing them up for the game.

For the first time Jamie understood what the pundits meant when they said a player would "run through brick walls".

Harry Armstrong was so brave he would make the brick wall feel scared!

The only Hawkstone player who didn't seem to be particularly interested in the warm-up was the goalkeeper, Leon Tibbs.

Tibbs was a bit of a Hawkstone legend, but in the last few seasons there was no doubt he'd put on some weight. And he was rude to the fans too. Jamie and Jack had once seen him in the street and asked for his autograph. Tibbs had just laughed at them and said, "You two couldn't afford *my* signature!"

Jamie could see that Tibbs wasn't even allowing the mascot to take proper shots at him. The mascot looked so scared that he wasn't even confident enough to give the ball a proper kick. What was the point in that?!

"See if you can pick up some tips today for that game of yours against Kingfield in a couple of weeks," Mike said to Jamie as Hawkstone kicked off in front of them. "The bigger the game, the better you should play."

Jamie nodded and tried to force a smile.

He felt bad because, on the way to the ground, he'd told Mike about his big upcoming school match against Kingfield – The Grove's fiercest rivals. Jamie had explained that it was the biggest match of the whole season and that sometimes the local newspaper even did a report on the game… And then Jamie had asked Mike not to come!

"Sometimes knowing that you're watching makes me a bit nervous," Jamie had said, trying to put into words why Mike had to stay away. "I just end up trying to impress you and then I don't play my normal game."

He'd been worried about Mike's reaction because he knew how much Mike loved to watch him play. But Mike had just said, "No worries. Whatever makes you happy, JJ."

That was why Jamie respected Mike so much: he always understood.

They got back home from the game to find a note from Jamie's mum on the kitchen table.

Hiya Dad and Jamie,

Did you have a good game? I heard you won! Does that mean you'll be in a good mood tomorrow then?

I'm popping out to meet Jeremy from work. And no, before either of you ask, it's not a date! We're just friends!!

Anyway there is food in the fridge. Have fun you two mischeif-makers!!

Love Mum/Karen xx

Jamie and Mike immediately did a high five. They were both stuffed from the fish and chips on the way home, but the fact that Jamie's mum was out meant that they didn't have to pretend they were still hungry!

They sat on the sofa, and, while Mike watched the golf, Jamie started reading the match programme from that day's game. He'd bought it with his own money. He always did whenever he went to a game, and he kept all the ones he'd ever bought. After every game, as soon as he got home, he read it from cover to cover, memorizing every word. Every fact.

It was strange, really. At school, Jamie hated reading. All his teachers spent their whole time trying to get him to read. But they wanted him to read about boring stuff like wars and poetry. If they'd just given him a Hawkstone programme, he could have read it quicker than anyone else. And sometimes he even learned good words from them too. Like "prodigy". That meant someone who had amazing skills.

Jamie wanted to be a football prodigy ... playing for Hawkstone United ... destined for the big time...

In the centre pages of the programme, there was a wicked poster of Harry Armstrong. Jamie carefully opened the staples and pulled it out, making sure not to rip it. He was going to stick it on his wall, alongside all the other Harry Armstrong posters he already had.

At the front of the programme, there was also a message from the Hawkstone chairman, Tony Walsh.

Jamie always read Tony Walsh's message to the fans because it was the only way he found out what the chairman's plans were for the club. Tony Walsh never did interviews on the TV, so Jamie didn't even know what he looked like! From what Jamie could tell from the programme, though, he seemed like a good bloke.

HAWKSTONE UNITED

CHAIRMAN'S ADDRESS

By Tony Walsh

...I'm delighted to say that our big Cup game against Tolford in a couple of weeks has already completely sold out.

With your fantastic support behind us, plus our plans to sign some of the best players from around the world, I believe that we are on schedule to achieve our aim of Champions League football for Hawkstone within the next five years.

Together we can do it.

I may be the chairman, but this will always be your Club.

Tony Walsh
Chairman
Hawkstone United Football Club

03

SATURDAY OCTOBER 16TH

Jamie closed his eyes and imagined his dream world. One day, he would be playing for Hawkstone United in the Champions League. He could see himself doing it... he wanted it so badly. *Make it happen,* he said to himself and anyone else who could hear his thoughts. *Please... make it happen.*

6

Two On Two

Sunday 17 October

As he sprinted down to meet his best mate, Jack, for their weekly kickaround, Jamie ran over yesterday's Hawkstone game in his mind.

Glenn Richardson had scored the only goal of the game with a wicked half-volley from the edge of the area. Hawkstone were having a seriously good season. They were even pushing for a European place.

But for Jamie, almost as interesting as watching the game had been watching Mike *watching* the game.

Jamie had tracked his reactions to everything that had happened to see if he could pick up any tips. After all, it wasn't as though many people had a granddad who had been a professional.

Generally, Mike didn't say much while the game was going on; he just chewed his gum and clapped the occasional pass, explaining to Jamie how the player had leant back so the ball went higher in the air or how he had used the outside of his boot to put more spin on the pass. Sometimes he just pointed to a spare man who was making a run, as though the Hawkstone players would somehow be able to telepathically pick up his suggestion.

The only time Mike had got really angry was when one of the opposition players pretended he had been fouled to try and get one of Hawkstone's players sent off. As the player was writhing around on the ground, faking an injury, Mike had got up out of his seat and shouted, "Get on with the game, you cheat!"

A few minutes later, after he'd chilled out a bit, he'd turned to Jamie and said, "I hope you never do that, JJ. A bit of class goes a long way in this game – remember that."

"Here he is," said Jack, as Jamie arrived in Sunningdale Park. "The man they're all talking about!"

"What d'you mean?" asked Jamie, blasting the ball at Jack, who was already in goal with her gloves on. "Who's talking about me?"

"The boys in the team at Kingfield," she said. "They've all heard of you. They were discussing how they're going to stop you in the match... Apparently they've made a special plan to put you off your game!"

"Tell them not to bother," smiled Jamie, bending in a shot. "No one's managed to stop me yet!"

"It's seriously wicked at Kingfield, you know," Jack called as she dived away to her right. She was a good 'keeper: brave and agile. "You should definitely ask your mum again about moving schools – you'd love it there. How's this week been at The Grove? Any better?"

Jamie was desperate to join Kingfield but, right now, his pride wouldn't let him admit it to Jack.

"Yeah, much better," Jamie lied. "You know those two bullies that I was telling you about?

Well, I taught them a lesson on Friday. I'd just had enough, so I sorted them both out. They were crying like babies at the end ... you should've seen it!"

"Really?" said Jack, a little surprised. "You took on both of 'em?"

"Course I did!" insisted Jamie. "Took 'em both down!"

"Wow," said Jack, taking off her gloves. "You must be really strong. Let me feel your muscles then!"

"Nah – get off!" said Jamie as Jack started tickling him in his armpit. "Jack! Get off me!" he squealed with a mixture of pleasure and pain as she continued. His laugh was so high-pitched, but he couldn't stop himself from giggling.

But then something made Jamie shut his mouth. His voice caught in his throat.

On the far side of the park, walking straight towards him and Jack, were Bryn Staunton and Tyler Forbes.

They were kicking a ball to each other, looking pretty hard as they strode forward. When they teamed up together they made a pretty menacing pair.

In the beginning, when he'd first joined The Grove, Jamie had sucked up to them to try and get in their gang but, because he played in the same position as Tyler, they weren't having any of it. They had decided that he was enemy number one.

And now after he'd got the better of them with the sickballs on Friday, they were out for revenge.

"Let's go," said Jamie, panicking as he turned to face Jack.

"Go? We've only just got here! What you chatting about?" she laughed. "Scared you won't be able to score against me, are you? Worried you're gonna flop?!"

"I'm serious, Jack! We need to go! Remember those two that I said I took down? Well, now they're coming here and they're gonna—"

But it was too late.

Bryn and Tyler had arrived.

"Playing with a girl, eh?" mocked Bryn. "Yeah, that's about all you're good enough for!"

"You're gonna get some beats on Monday, man ... you best believe!" threatened Tyler, smacking his fist into his hand as Jamie started to back away.

"OK," Jack said suddenly, surprising all three of the boys. "How's about we sort this out with a quick game of two on two?"

"Against you two? A midget and a girl! We'll destroy you," laughed Bryn.

"Maybe you will," smiled Jack, calmly. "But, if we win, you leave Jamie alone. Deal?"

"If you win, I'll run down the street naked!" shouted Bryn. Then he and Tyler started laughing, giving each other high fives.

"Er, I don't think anyone wants to see that," countered Jack. "Look, deal or no deal?"

"I'll tell you what the deal is," Bryn snapped, coming up right next to Jack and Jamie, aggressively staring them both in the eye. "You win – fine, we leave him alone, won't touch him no more... but if we win, he never plays football at school again. Ever. And Tyler takes his place in the school team."

"Nice one, bruv!" said Tyler, touching fists with Bryn.

"So that's the deal," Bryn said, turning back to Jack. "You still want it?"

"That doesn't even make sense," Jamie interrupted. He was getting annoyed at everyone talking about him as though he wasn't there. "What do I tell the coach when he asks why I'm not playing? And what sport am I supposed to do if I don't play football?"

"Who cares?" said Bryn. "That's your problem."

"How about basketball?!" teased Tyler. They both collapsed into laughter again at the thought of little Jamie Johnson trying to do a slam-dunk!

"Well, then?" asked Bryn impatiently. "What's it gonna be?"

Jamie and Jack looked at each other. Jamie shook his head. It was too big a risk. He *had* to be able to play football at school. It was what he lived for and his best chance of getting a professional club to spot his talent.

"Deal!" said Jack, completely ignoring Jamie. "Let's do it."

"What are you doing?" Jamie whispered angrily to Jack as they retreated into their own territory to organize their goal with their jumpers. "If I can't play football at school, I may as well—"

"Chill out, will ya, JJ?" said Jack, confidently bouncing the ball down on the ground. "What are you worried about? You sorted 'em out at school. Now you can sort 'em out again!"

"Jack, I was lying, it wasn't exactly like I—"

"Come on, JJ!" said Jack. "How many times have we ever lost a two v two?"

They looked at each other and then Jamie grinned.

"Never," he smiled.

7
Sunday Best

Right from the very first kick of the match, when Jamie flicked the ball into the air, did an around-the-world, then back-heeled it to Jack, Bryn and Tyler simply could not get the ball off Jamie.

Even when the two of them paired up to both man-to-man mark him, it made no difference!

He was too quick, too skilful, too agile … too good.

The score had reached 12-1 before an exhausted Bryn Staunton finally said the magic words.

"All right, fair play, you win," he conceded, shaking Jack and Jamie's hands. "We'll leave the guy alone. And Tyler, I ain't being funny, mate, but I reckon you should find a new position. You ain't ever going to be as good as Jamie. He's got some serious skills!"

That Sunday afternoon, perhaps for the first time, Bryn Staunton and Tyler Forbes began to fully understand the talent that Jamie Johnson had for football.

This was not a normal boy. This was not just *some kid who* liked to play football.

This was a very special talent, and to take it on – to try to beat it – was stupid, not to say impossible.

Jamie didn't say a word to them after the game. There was no need. His feet had done all the talking.

Together, Jamie and Jack hadn't just beaten Bryn and Tyler; they had destroyed them.

After Bryn and Tyler had gone, Jamie and Jack sat down on their favourite bench to bask in their victory. They had had some good wins in Sunningdale but none as satisfying as this. Bryn had even asked Jamie to play on his side in break next week.

And Jamie knew that none of this would have happened had it not been for Jack. He had been ready to run away. It was only because she'd stood up to them that Jamie had had the confidence to do the same.

"Here," said Jamie. "Give me your key ring for a sec."

"What for?"

"Just give it here, will you?"

When Jack handed it over, Jamie pointed the sharp edge at the wood and, very carefully, started etching some letters into the bench.

J+J 4EVER, he carved.

As he went to bed that night, in his mind Jamie replayed some of the moves that he'd used in the match against Bryn and Tyler. In particular, he was pleased with the nutmeg he'd done on Tyler on his way to slotting home one of the 11 goals he'd scored in the game.

The nutmeg had been so perfect that even Bryn had shouted *"Nuts!"* And he was on Tyler's team!

Jamie reached over to set his alarm for school. It was 10.30pm on a Sunday night. Normally at this time, his stomach would be tight, and he would be nervously anticipating going back to school the next morning, dreading that buzzer going off and the journey to The Grove in the freezing morning fog.

But tonight, Jamie had none of those worries. In fact, after the lesson he'd taught Bryn and Tyler on the football pitch this weekend and then Bryn's invitation for him to play on their side in break, Jamie was actually looking forward to school tomorrow. Well, almost, anyway…

8

Turning The Tables

Monday 18 October

"Oi, Jamie! Over here!"

Jamie had his tray and was looking for somewhere to sit at lunch. He heard someone calling his name but he didn't know where in the dining hall the voice was coming from. Then Bryn got up off his bench and started flailing his arms around to catch his attention.

"Jamie!" he shouted again. "Over here!"

This is beautiful, Jamie thought to himself as he carried his tray over, *seriously beautiful.*

"Oi, shift up, will you?" Bryn said to Tyler. "He needs some room to sit down."

As soon as Jamie sat down, the talk turned to the match against Kingfield School, which was only just over a week away now.

"We gotta do 'em!" announced Bryn. "They reckon they're so hard. We gotta teach them a lesson!"

Jamie looked to the end of the table and saw Shaun McGiven eating his lunch in silence. McGiven was probably the quietest boy in the whole year. His skin was so pale that sometimes he reminded Jamie of a ghost. But if you put that boy on a football pitch, he was guaranteed to score you a goal. He was the best striker Jamie had ever played with.

"Oi, Bryn," said Jamie, suddenly feeling pumped with confidence. "Don't worry about Kingfield, mate. Just give me and McGiven the ball and we'll do the rest!"

All the boys started laughing and punching their fists on the table.

Jamie smiled. It felt good to be on the inside.

There was only one problem, and Jamie knew he'd have to sort it out sooner or later.

Hugo Bogson.

Thursday 21 October

After school on Thursday, Bryn, Jamie and the rest of the boys were all standing at the bus stop waiting to catch the bus into town to go to the arcade when Hugo Bogson started walking towards them.

He even walked in a slightly weird way, bouncing a little too high off the ground, almost as though he were skipping.

"Do you want to come over to mine?" Hugo asked Jamie as the bus drew nearer.

Jamie could already hear the muffled laughter that Hugo's presence had brought about from the rest of the gang. They thought Hugo was a complete idiot. He'd heard them refer to Boggy as a "mentalist" and "freak boy".

Jamie knew that this was an important moment. He'd just got in with the others and, together, they had won every match at break-time this week. He was starting to get really popular. He couldn't blow it now.

"Come over to yours?" Jamie said. "No way! Your house stinks, man!"

Jamie turned and did high fives with everyone. They couldn't stop laughing as they watched Hugo Bogson walk away, head down, with his feet now barely lifting off the ground.

But even while he was still laughing, as he watched Hugo disappear out of sight, Jamie couldn't help but feel a little bit guilty at the same time.

9

The Overhead Kick

Sunday 24 October

"I'm telling you, we've got some seriously good players!" Jack was saying as the banter ahead of The Grove-Kingfield match notched up another gear. The game was only two days away now and it was all they had talked about this weekend.

"Our captain, right, Dillon Simmonds, is the hardest player I've ever seen," Jack boasted. "I reckon he eats glass for breakfast! And Ollie, our midfielder, is seriously brave. He's a good guy too. I reckon you'd like him."

Jamie didn't like the thought of Jack having other friends. Especially ones that he didn't know.

"Plus we've got a wicked striker," Jack continued, saving one of Jamie's long-range lobs. "He's called Ash. You should tell your defenders to watch out for him! He's the quickest runner in the whole of our year... He's almost as quick as you!"

Jamie smiled. He liked it when Jack gave him compliments. But it was true. He'd never yet met anyone who was as fast as him. Sometimes he wondered if anyone was!

"Yeah, well, bet he doesn't score as many goals as Shaun McGiven!" Jamie hit back. "That boy is a killer in the area, I'm telling you."

"Bet he does!" Jack shot back. "Ash can do overhead kicks! He's even taught me how to do them!"

"Yeah, right!" laughed Jamie.

They'd been playing in the park together for years, and neither of them had ever managed to do a proper overhead kick. They'd always ended up falling on their backs and laughing through the pain at how rubbish their attempts had been.

"I can't even do an overhead kick and I'm a *winger,*" said Jamie. "You're only a 'keeper!"

"Wanna bet?" Jack challenged. "Milkshakes?"

"Done," said Jamie. Only now was he starting to have any doubts – Jack always won their bets. Still, he could hardly imagine that Jack had learned how to do an overhead kick. This bet had to be his. He'd get an extra large milkshake to teach her a lesson.

They spat on their hands and shook them.

And then, without saying another word. Jack tossed the ball into the air and, as it dropped, she launched her body towards it.

And sure enough, like a legend, she produced the most amazing overhead kick. It was an absolutely perfect strike... the ball went miles!

"No way!" Jamie shouted. "Do it again!"

"Why?" laughed Jack, leaping back up to her feet. She didn't seem to be hurt at all. "You think it was a fluke?!"

"Just do it again. That was the best overhead kick I've ever seen. Go on! Do it!"

And so, just like before, Jack tossed the ball into the air and produced an awesome overhead kick! It didn't even look like she was trying.

"OK, you have to teach me!" Jamie begged, with a mixture of jealousy and excitement. "I'm serious! Teach me now! Please!"

"OK, but only if you promise not to use it against Kingfield – Ash'll kill me otherwise!"

"I promise ... whatever! I just have to learn how to do that!"

"Fine," said Jack. "But when you're a big star and everything, you remember who taught you how to do an overhead kick!"

Jamie smiled while Jack picked up the ball and talked him through exactly how to do the manoeuvre.

"See, at the moment you're too worried about hitting the ground when you come back down. You're thinking about that instead of focusing on the ball," she explained.

"You've just got to relax," she continued. "It's all in the timing. Trust me."

"As the ball comes to you, leave your kicking leg on the ground and jump into the air, leading with your other leg…"

"Then, keep your eyes completely fixed on the ball, right through until you strike it..."

"Strike the ball with your laces... and still keep your eyes on it."

"Then, after you've got in your shot, just use your arms to break your fall. That way, you'll be up quickly to celebrate your goal!"

10

Standing Up

Monday 25 October

Jamie was just telling Bryn and Tyler about his overhead kicks when, out of the corner of his eye, he saw Hugo Bogson walking around the dining hall with his tray piled high with ravioli. The gloopy red sauce was trickling over the side of his plate.

Jamie could see Hugo's eyes scanning the room. Then, as he spotted Jamie, his eyes lit up and he hurried towards him, like a faithful dog that has just spotted its owner.

But Jamie looked away and carried on talking to Bryn.

"You can do overhead kicks?!" Bryn was saying. "Seriously? Show us how to do them, then!"

Jamie was only partially concentrating on the conversation because the rest of his brain was registering the fact that, at the last minute, Hugo had veered away from Jamie's table.

Finally, Jamie thought to himself. *Finally, he's got the message.*

It was harsh – and Jamie couldn't help feeling a bit sorry for Hugo, who was sitting all by himself on the other side of the dining hall – but things had changed now and the sooner Hugo understood that, the bet—

"Oi, Jamie!" Bryn was half-shouting now. "So are you gonna show us how to do overhead kicks or what?!"

Match v Kingfield tomorrow.
Kick-off 2.30p.m
Coach leaves at 1p.m. from the front gate.
Clean kits, please!
Mr Bolitho

Jamie read the notice three times and wrote down all the details in his school diary. He had to be right on time for tomorrow. Preparation was everything.

Jamie looked at his watch and sprinted to class for English but, even though he was four minutes late, the teacher was not there yet.

It was 2.04pm and, with no sign of Mr Leyburn, everyone was starting to mess around. It was almost like a party in the classroom.

Bryn was jeering loudly as Hugo Bogson went around the class trying to find a spare seat. Every time he tried to sit down next to someone, they simply said, "Sorry, this seat's taken."

Finally, Hugo found a seat at the front, right next to the teacher's desk.

He took off his rucksack and went to sit down, but, just before his bum connected with the chair, Bryn whipped it away.

Hugo went crashing to the floor and, as he hit the deck, the whole class erupted in thunderous laughter.

Then, while Hugo was vulnerable, Bryn and Tyler piled in to pinch him on his cheek and his bum.

"Enjoy your trip?!" they mocked, pinching away painfully at him and flicking his ears.

"Get off," Hugo protested, trying in vain to push their hands away. "Leave me alone! What have I done to you?"

"What's the matter?" shouted Bryn. "We're only having a laugh! Can't the weirdo take a joke?!"

Now they were emptying Hugo's rucksack and tipping the contents all over the floor.

"OK, enough now," Jamie said, suddenly standing up. He knew this wasn't right.

Bryn and Tyler looked up at him. Then they started laughing and continued where they had left off.

"Hold him down, Tyler," shouted Bryn excitedly. "I'm gonna fart on his head!"

"I mean it, guys. Leave him alone," Jamie repeated firmly.

Bryn stood up and walked towards Jamie. Jamie took half a step back. He wondered if things were about to go back to the bad old days.

"And what do you care about freak boy for anyway, Johnson?" he barked. "You don't have to pretend to be his mate anymore now!"

"He's all right," said Jamie, standing up as tall as he could. He came up to Bryn's neck. "He's not done anything to you lot."

"Yes, he has!" shouted Tyler, who now had Hugo in a headlock. "He's offended me with his BO! He smells like a tramp!"

"Well, I think he's all right," countered Jamie. "So you better leave him alone!"

"Or what?" Tyler bellowed. This was getting serious now.

"Yeah," said Bryn. "Or what?"

Jamie's mind suddenly went horribly blank. *Or what?!* He didn't know the answer to that question. What could he possibly threaten Bryn and Tyler with? He tried to imagine what Jack would do in this situation. She never lost her cool…

"Or I don't teach you overhead kicks and I'll never play on your team in break ever again,"

Jamie suddenly blurted out with as much confidence as he could muster. He wondered if they could see his chest pounding through his shirt. He could feel his heart racing.

Tyler looked to Bryn and Bryn looked to Jamie. Jamie nodded to show he was serious.

For a couple of seconds there was absolute silence.

Then Bryn stormed up to Hugo and pulled his clenched fist back. Hugo flinched, preparing himself for the punch that would knock him out. But instead, he only felt Bryn's arm sweep around his neck in a kind of brotherly embrace.

"What are you worried for, Boggy, me old chum?" said Bryn, slapping Hugo very hard on his back. "Like Jamie says... you're all right by us..."

11

Match Day

Tuesday 26 October

KINGFIELD V THE GROVE

KICK-OFF 2.30

12.55 p.m.

Jamie was just getting on the coach to go to the match against Kingfield when he heard his name being called.

At first Jamie ignored it because he recognized the voice. But the calls kept coming.

"Jamie! Wait!" Hugo Bogson was shouting. He was so near now that it was impossible for

Jamie not to acknowledge him. He just hoped Hugo didn't embarrass him in front of everyone before the game. He needed all his confidence for this match.

"Hugo," said Jamie, turning around and getting off the coach. "I'm in a rush, mate, we're just about to go to the—"

"I wanted to give you something," said Hugo, rummaging around in the bottom of his rucksack.

"Sorry, mate, I haven't got time," said Jamie. He wondered what kind of rubbish rested at the bottom of Hugo's rucksack. "We're leaving right now."

"Here you go!" said Hugo triumphantly, handing Jamie a package in a plastic bag. "These are for you."

"What is it?" asked Jamie suspiciously as he took hold of the package. If it was some of Hugo's "special" sandwiches, he might be sick on the spot.

"Open it!" smiled Hugo.

Jamie nodded and, very slowly, with extreme caution, he peered inside the plastic bag. Then he pulled out the contents.

He couldn't believe it.

In his hands, he was holding a brand new pair of shin pads. They were the best ones on the market.

"Wow!" said Jamie. "Why are you giving me these, Hugo? Not that I don't like them... or need them... they're sick—"

"Way I see it," said Hugo, "you stopped me from getting a kicking yesterday... thought maybe I could do the same for you today."

"I'll wear these for the match today!" smiled Jamie. "Thanks, Hugo."

"Pleasure," replied Hugo. "Now pull my finger!"

As Jamie stepped off the coach, arriving at Kingfield's pitches, he felt the same sensations in his body that he felt before every big game: a tingling combination of confidence, fear and excitement. The anticipation bubbled in his blood and the longing for a win – the need to succeed – tantalized his mind.

But today, the quickening of his pulse, the sudden shot of adrenaline into his veins seemed to be sending Jamie the message that something extra, something different, might be afoot.

He sensed that today was going to be an important day in his football career. A special day, even.

The question was, why? And… how?

12

Game On!

"Hi," said a player on the Kingfield team, as Jamie jogged out on to the pitch. He was the biggest boy Jamie had ever seen. Was he really only in Year Seven?

"My name's Dillon Simmonds," the boy said, politely, shaking Jamie's hand. "Listen, I've just lost one of my contact lenses. I was wondering if you could help me find it?"

"Sure," said Jamie, surprised at how nice this Dillon boy seemed. Maybe Jamie could even become mates with a couple of the Kingfield players.

Jamie got down and started looking in the grass for the contact lens. He was really good at finding things, so he was sure he would be able to help Dillon find his lens. Then Jamie realized he had been a bit rude; he hadn't even introduced himself!

"Oh, my name's Jamie, by the—"

Thump! Dillon Simmonds kicked Jamie really hard up his bum, sending him tumbling over on to his back.

"What did you do that for?" Jamie yelled. His bum really hurt. "I was just trying to—"

"I don't even wear contact lenses, you idiot!" Dillon howled with laughter. "And that's only the first time I'm gonna kick you today!"

"What's your problem?" said Jamie, getting up. He looked around him to see if there was any backup. There was none.

"You're my problem!" shouted Dillon, leering over him. "Oh, are you standing up now? I couldn't even tell! Why you so small then? Is your dad a dwarf?!"

"Don't talk about my dad!" Jamie snarled. "You don't know nothing about my dad!"

Jamie was so angry now, he wanted to punch this ugly idiot as hard as he could, right in the face.

"OOOOOOH! Raw nerve!!" laughed Dillon, walking back to the changing rooms. "Sorry to upset you, dwarf boy! See you out on the pitch!"

Jamie watched him go.

You'll pay for that, Dillon Simmonds, he promised himself. *You'll pay.*

13

Action Time

KINGFIELD 1 - 1 THE GROVE

A KHAN, 7 S MCGIVEN, 16

58 MINS PLAYED

Jamie had to admit it. This was one of the toughest matches he'd ever played.

Normally The Grove were way better than the other schools they came up against. With Jamie Johnson and Shaun McGiven up front, they had too much firepower for most teams to handle.

But today was different. Today, The Grove had come up against a team that were just as good as they were. It was going to be a seriously close game and everyone knew it.

Kingfield had taken an early lead through their top striker, Ashish Khan. Jack had warned Jamie about him and she had been right. He could seriously shift. He'd outpaced the entire Grove back line before sending a cheeky chip home to open the scoring.

But then, like any good team. The Grove had hit back quickly. Jamie had dribbled past four players and set up Shaun McGiven, who equalized with a trademark curler into the top corner.

And since then, the game had been really tight.

Even Jamie was finding it hard to make an impression. The main reason for that was Dillon Simmonds.

He was tracking Jamie wherever he went and if he wasn't putting in dangerous, crunching tackles, he was taunting and teasing Jamie with his verbals. It was as though he really hated Jamie, even though this was the first time they had ever met each other.

"Oi, muppet, where did ya get those boots? The charity shop? Can't you afford a proper pair?" Dillon Simmonds smirked as he made a run past Jamie towards The Grove's goal. Didn't he know that defenders were supposed to stay at the back?

Jamie hadn't reacted to any of Dillon's cusses yet. He knew his time would come. He just had to wait. Until the time was right. Then he would show Dillon what true talent was. Show him that skill was way more powerful than brute for—

Suddenly, the ball had rebounded to Dillon, who was standing 35 yards from The Grove's goal. Dillon powered forward, controlling the ball firmly on his chest. The ball bounced up above his head and then, as it dropped out of nowhere, Dillon pelted a ferocious left-foot volley at the goal. It was a massive strike ... and it was on target!

Jamie couldn't bear to watch. As soon as the ball had been struck he could tell it was going to go all the way. It was way too hard and far too high for The Grove 'keeper to get anywhere near it.

It shot like a rocket straight into the top corner.

Dillon Simmonds, the big, stupid, psycho defender, had just scored an unbelievable solo goal. And didn't he know it...

KINGFIELD 2 - 1 THE GROVE

A KHAN, 7 | S MCGIVEN, 16
D SIMMONDS, 61

"Come on!!" Dillon shouted, his cheeks burning red with glory. He'd raced over to the corner flag and kicked it way out of the ground to celebrate his amazing goal.

"What do you think about that, then?!" he roared at The Grove players. "Have some of that!"

The Grove were losing.

Jamie hated losing. At anything. It didn't matter what it was: a game of cards, snakes and ladders, a computer game. Whatever he did, he had to win. But most of all, what he couldn't bear, what he couldn't accept, was losing at football.

Once, when Jamie had lost a big Cup game at his primary school, he had been so angry and upset that he hadn't eaten a thing for the rest of the day. His mum had got really cross, telling him that he was going to make himself ill, but Jamie had just ignored her. She didn't understand that losing at football was the worst thing in the world.

It started a rage in Jamie. A rage that could only be calmed by him proving them wrong. Him proving that *he* was number one. He was the best.

Now, as the ball bounced towards him, Jamie knew it was time for him to do something.

He gathered in the ball and went on a run…

As soon as he had the ball under control, Jamie's mind instantly rid itself of all the clutter that normally littered it. Now, with the ball at his feet, Jamie's brain was clear and free. Free for football. Programmed to play. Set to score.

Jamie turned on his turbo gear and raced forward with the speed of a panther.

He'd already sped past three players and was heading right for the heart of the Kingfield defence when Dillon Simmonds slashed him down with a violent foul.

Jamie had been stopped. But not for long.

Because now he had exactly what he wanted.

A free kick…

14

A Big Decision

KINGFIELD 2 - 1 THE GROVE

A KHAN, 7   S MCGIVEN, 16
D SIMMONDS, 61

67 MINS PLAYED

Jamie addressed the ball straight on. Then he took three steps back, stood up to his full height and puffed out his chest. He took a series of deep breaths as he visualized exactly what he wanted to do with this free kick.

It was a fair way out – 22 yards from goal – so Jamie knew he had to go for swerve and power rather than curl and accuracy.

Jamie stared hard at the ball. He was thinking about Luiz Rodriguez. Rodriguez was a Portuguese winger and the best free kick taker in the world. Jamie had spent the whole of last week watching his free kicks on YouTube.

Watching the free kicks in slow-motion, Jamie had noticed that, when he struck the ball, Rodriguez never used a full follow-through. He punched his boot ferociously through the ball but then, as soon as possible after he had made contact, he brought his foot back down to the ground. This seemed to unleash a movement in the ball that no other technique could produce. Perhaps it was something to do with the pressure in the ball. Either way, it was almost impossible to stop.

Now it was Jamie's turn to have a go.

Jamie took a deep, determined breath, followed by three powerful strides towards the ball.

Then he hit it with the maximum force his body possessed. He struck the ball perfectly on its valve, bringing his foot quickly back down to the ground after it had made contact.

Now, Jamie just stood and watched. He'd done his bit. The rest was up to the ball.

All the players on the pitch – and even the referee – were hypnotized by the movement of the ball in the air. They watched it arc towards its target.

The goalkeeper stood, paralysed, on his line, his feet anchored to the ground. Jamie actually felt a bit sorry for him. How could you try to save a ball when you had no idea which direction it was going to move next?

Thwack! The ball hit the goalkeeper's right-hand post, halfway up. Now it was spinning furiously across the goal-line. Was it going to go in? Or was it – *thud!* It hit the other post ... And it bounced out!

It was unbelievable. None of the players had ever seen a shot hit *both* posts and then bounce out without going in! Every player stood open-mouthed, trying to work out the science of how it had actually been possible.

Every player, that is, apart from Shaun McGiven. He was already on the move. He chased smoothly and swiftly after the ball, catching it in an instant. He hungrily gobbled up the chance, clipping the ball home with a quick, powerful strike before anyone else had moved.

That's what made McGiven different from other players. He was a true finisher. A natural-born predator. And he'd just scored again!

KINGFIELD 2 - 2 THE GROVE

A KHAN, 7 — S MCGIVEN, 16, 68
D SIMMONDS, 61

Even though it was McGiven's name on the scoresheet, Jamie still raised his arms proudly above his head in triumph. He nodded confidently in appreciation of his own skill. He even looked up to the sky in some form of acknowledgement. He knew that no one else on the pitch was capable of doing what he had just done with the football.

Suddenly, Jamie felt his whole body being hoisted into the air.

"What a free kick, Jamie!" Bryn Staunton was shouting. His bear hug from behind had lifted Jamie four feet off the ground! "That was just like Rodriguez! Awesome!"

"Course it was!" said Jamie, as Bryn finally put him down. "I taught him everything he knows!"

There were 10 minutes of the match left and both teams were piling forward in search of the winner. There was glory on offer for whoever could snatch the final goal.

Jamie was desperate to get on the scoresheet himself and win the game for The Grove. He had a feeling that he still had a big role to play in this match. But as time ticked on, it was Kingfield who looked more and more likely to score a goal.

They had a corner.

"You all go up," Dillon Simmonds ordered his Kingfield teammates. "Don't worry about the ugly muppet; I'll handle him!"

Jamie was getting more and more angry but, if he could just get on the ball, he knew he could tear Dillon to shreds. However, right now, the action was all happening at the other end.

As the corner was whipped into the centre of the area, Bryn Staunton and one of the Kingfield players rose to contest it in the air. It was a 50-50 tussle and, although the Kingfield player made the first connection with the ball, they clashed heads badly. It sounded like two coconuts being crashed together.

Jamie saw the Kingfield player slump to the ground. He looked in a really bad way but the ball had been cleared straight to Jamie.

With everyone committed to the corner, there were only two outfield players in the Kingfield half. One big, strong defender called Dillon Simmonds and one small, swift, skilful winger called Jamie Johnson.

Now was the time. The time for Jamie to let his talent come tumbling out.

Jamie latched on to the ball and immediately turned to face Dillon Simmonds.

Then he channelled all his anger at Dillon into his legs and burst forward with the ball. He was travelling at his very top speed, jinking left and right, with amazing close skill.

Now the tables had turned; Jamie was the one who was teasing Dillon. But he was doing it with the ball. His pace and control was mesmerizing the big defender, who suddenly seemed to be struggling to even stay on his feet.

This way and that Jamie turned, each time slipping away from Dillon's lunges. Jamie was like a wet bar of soap that Dillon could never quite catch.

He wasn't just one step ahead of Dillon Simmonds; he was light years in front.

Finally, Jamie flew past Dillon. Dillon tried to kick him – of course he did – but the impact of his boot had no effect on Jamie. The shin pads protected him perfectly.

Now Jamie bore down towards the goal. He only had to decide how he was going to finish this game whether he would go around the 'keeper with the ball or just slot it past him from the edge of the area.

"Bang it! Shoot!" Jamie's teammates from The Grove were shouting. They knew Jamie never missed a one on one.

But while his teammates were yelling at the top of their voices, Jamie had noticed that the crowd on the sidelines had gone deadly quiet.

In fact, they weren't even watching the game; they were pointing back towards The Grove's penalty area. There was worry on their faces.

Jamie turned around to see that the Kingfield player who had gone up for the header from the corner was still lying on the ground. He hadn't moved.

Jamie knew something was not right. If players were rolling around in agony, it meant they were in pain, but if they were not moving, it meant that they might not even be conscious…

Almost without thinking, Jamie kicked the ball straight out of play. Yes, he was giving up a near-certain goal, but he knew that boy needed help.

As soon as the ball went out, a man sprinted onto the pitch towards the stricken boy. "Does anyone here know first aid?" he shouted. There was panic in his voice.

15

A Touch of Class

KINGFIELD 2 - 2 THE GROVE

A KHAN, 7 | S MCGIVEN, 16, 68
D SIMMONDS, 61

FULL TIME

The game had finished in a draw. A bit of Jamie couldn't help but wonder if he'd done the right thing.

He had had the glory there in his grip. One kick and he could have won the game. He might even have got his name in the paper. But at the same time, he knew that something really bad could have happened to that boy.

He'd call Mike on the way home to ask him whether he'd done the right thing. He hoped Mike would back him up. After all, he was the one who always told Jamie how important sportsmanship was...

A little cloud of sadness hovered over Jamie for a second. He wished Mike had been here to watch the game.

But there was no need for Jamie to have worried...

Mike had been at the match all right – he'd had to wear a baseball cap and stand way over on the other side of the pitch, but there was no way he was going to miss watching Jamie play in a game like this.

And, leaving the Kingfield grounds before anyone could recognize him, Mike had a very big smile on his face.

This match had proved something to him that, deep down, he had probably always known...

His grandson had both the talent and the character to be a very special footballer indeed.

Out in the car park, Jamie was just putting his

new shin pads into his kitbag when he sensed someone's large presence loom next to him.

Jamie tensed his stomach muscles. What if it was Dillon coming to do him in?

"I think my son and I owe you a thank you … Jamie, is it?"

It was the man who had run on to the pitch to help the boy who'd got injured. He had on the nicest coat Jamie had ever seen.

"No probs," said Jamie. "Is he OK? Looked like a bad one."

"Ollie's fine." The man smiled. "But it could have been serious. The blow to his head knocked him clean out and his tongue was blocking his airway… It's just lucky you kicked the ball out when you did. Is there any way I can thank you?"

"It's fine," said Jamie. "Don't worry about it. I'm just glad he's OK."

"No, really. I mean it – it was a real touch of class, what you did… Trust me, I'll think of something," he said, getting into his car. It was a brand new Ferrari and it had the personalized number plate

Jamie stared at the car in awe. He wondered if he would ever get to just *sit* in a car like that, let alone own one!

"Hang on a minute," said the man, getting back out of his car. "Who do you support, Jamie?"

"Hawkstone United," said Jamie, proudly. "All the way."

"Good," smiled the man. "I was hoping you might say that ... and where are you planning to watch the Cup game tomorrow?"

"I'm going to go to my granddad's. We watch every game together..."

"You could do that," said the man. "Or you and your family could come to the game as my guests. How would you like to be Hawkstone's mascot, Jamie? I'm the chairman, by the way. My name's Tony Walsh."

16

Leading Out The Team

Wednesday 27 October

Just before he left the house to head to the Hawkstone ground, Jamie looked at himself in the mirror.

This was the face that 37,000 people would see on the pitch tonight.

Was he ugly, like that boy Dillon had said? Jamie didn't know the answer.

His mum had always told him that he was handsome and that the girls would be queuing up for him. But then again, she was his mum, she would hardly tell him he was ugly, would—

"Do we have a Hawkstone mascot in the house?!"

Jamie smiled as he registered Mike's voice booming up the stairs.

"Come on, JJ, let's get this show on the road!" He laughed as Jamie appeared at the top of the stairs. "I don't think they'll delay the kick-off, even for a VIP guest like you!"

As he waited in the tunnel for the Hawkstone players to come out of their dressing room, a flutter of nerves shivered through Jamie. He couldn't believe he was here, in this ground, at the club of his dreams. He had prayed for this moment to happen all his life.

"Hello, mate," said Harry Armstrong, the Hawkstone captain, who was the first out of the dressing room. He shook Jamie's hand and said, "What's your name? I'm Harry."

Jamie almost laughed. He knew who Harry Armstrong was – he was his biggest fan! But what he was struggling to come to terms with was the fact that he was now actually meeting Harry Armstrong ... *in real life.*

"I'm Jamie. Jamie Johnson."

"Nice to meet you, Jamie. So what do you want to be when you're older then?"

"I'm going to be a footballer," said Jamie, feeling his confidence rise. "I'm going to play for Hawkstone alongside you!"

Harry Armstrong laughed and ruffled Jamie's hair. "Good for you, kid," he smiled. "I'll look forward to it!"

Then the referee – who had a very bald head and very hairy legs – walked to the front of the line and shook hands with both captains. They all called each other by their first names, but none of them seemed like friends.

"Ready, lads, here we go!" bellowed Harry Armstrong.

Suddenly Harry grabbed Jamie's hand and began the walk out of the tunnel towards the pitch.

With every stride, the roar of the crowd got nearer and louder.

Now, as they strode out on to the pitch, the wall of noise belted Jamie's ears. It was the loudest sound he had ever heard.

At that moment, Jamie couldn't imagine that anything else was happening in the world.

It seemed that everyone on earth was here, shouting their heads off, ready for the big game!

As Jamie led the team out with Harry Armstrong, he knew for sure that he had never been happier in his life.

There were cameras, commentators and 37,000 people all focusing their attention directly on Jamie. But Jamie no longer felt nervous. In fact, he felt the reverse. Maths tests made him nervous. Not football.

As he kicked his first ball on the Hawkstone pitch, a set of words kept repeating themselves in Jamie's mind.

The words seemed to be coming from every cell in his body: "This is where I belong… This is where I belong…"

17

Playing To The Crowd

"Jamie! Coin toss!" shouted Harry Armstrong.

He had remembered Jamie's name! Harry Armstrong actually remembered Jamie's name!

As they walked to the centre circle to toss the coin with the opposition, Jamie realized that Harry Armstrong was a lot bigger in person than he seemed on the TV. Jamie knew everything about him – that he was five-foot eleven, and weighed twelve stone. He even knew when his birthday was! (October 13th.) But it was only now, standing next to him, that Jamie properly felt the physical presence that Harry Armstrong exuded.

Jamie saw the look of steel in Harry's eyes, which said that he would stop at nothing to achieve victory.

Jamie smiled. If Planet Earth was sending a football team to play against a team of aliens from outer space, he thought that Harry Armstrong should be Planet Earth's captain. That's how highly Jamie rated him.

While the photographer took a photo of Jamie and Harry Armstrong standing together by the centre spot, in the stands, Mike was filming every second.

"Don't worry about filming it, Dad," suggested Jamie's mum. "Just watch it – you'll enjoy it more."

Mike glanced at her and smiled. He was still using his old video camera even though the new phone that Jamie and his mum had bought him for his birthday had a wicked camera on it.

"It's not for *me,*" Mike said. "It's for Jamie. You never know – one day, he might thank me."

"OK, let's get this over and done with, kid," Leon Tibbs growled as Jamie jogged towards his goal. Hawkstone's grumpy 'keeper was chomping his way through a mouthful of gum as he rolled the ball out to Jamie's feet.

Jamie nodded and did the lightest kick he could back into Tibbs' hands. He was too scared to do anything else.

"That's it," Tibbs shouted. "Just a couple more. Then you can go back to your daddy and I can get a proper warm-up."

Jamie felt his temples bristle with sweat. He didn't like it when people underestimated him. And he liked it even less when they talked about his dad.

With the next ball, Jamie tried a curler, hitting the ball a bit harder this time. Tibbs only just got across to make the save.

"Don't you dare try and score against me, titch," snarled Tibbs. "You're not good enough. End of story!"

Jamie began to feel his adrenaline kicking in as he heard a few people in the crowd start to notice him.

Tibbs gave Jamie a stern look as he rolled the ball back out to him.

Jamie teed himself up for a volley this time and belted it as hard as he could! Tibbs flung himself into the air and pushed it wide with the very tips of his fingers. It was a great piece of action.

Some of the crowd even clapped.

"One more time, kid..." Tibbs threatened. "Just try it one more time, and believe me, you won't know what's hit you."

Jamie knew he shouldn't have done it, but he couldn't help it; the more the crowd clapped him, the more he wanted to please them.

Now Jamie did a chip. It was a beautiful little drifter of a shot which seemed to glide effortlessly through the air. Jamie could see the anger on Tibbs' face as he back-pedalled furiously to tip the ball on to the crossbar. Jamie had so nearly scored!

This was turning into a proper battle now and quite a few of the fans were getting to their feet to witness the contest.

Tibbs charged towards Jamie.

"See! I told you you'd never score against me! Now get off this pitch before I kick you off myself!" he yelled.

"OK! I'm going!" said Jamie. He could see the blood vessels in Tibbs's eyes starting to go red.

As Jamie started to walk off the pitch, some of the crowd even booed. They wanted him to stay on!

There was one more ball on the edge of the penalty area and Jamie was desperate to have another shot, but he knew that if he did, Tibbs would probably go so mental that he'd have a fit before the match had even started.

Jamie knew his time was up. He headed for the tunnel.

"Go home and ask your daddy to teach you some respect!" Leon Tibbs shouted after him.

Suddenly Jamie stopped walking. Now he was angry. Very angry.

Stuff you, Leon Tibbs, he thought to himself as he slowly turned around.

Then Jamie walked confidently up to the ball on the edge of the area and flicked it into the air, with his back still to goal. *You're the one who needs to learn some respect!*

Jamie controlled the ball on his chest, and let it fall back down to his thigh. Then he kneed it up into the air...

Focusing completely on the ball, Jamie launched his body up off the ground to meet it.

Jamie was lying completely flat in the air. His eyes were fixed firmly on the ball as he snapped first his right foot, then his left foot, back with ferocious pace over his head.

The contact was sweet and powerful. Hard and accurate. As Jamie dropped to the ground, the ball arrowed towards the goal. Jamie didn't even have to look around; he knew it was a beautiful overhead kick. His football senses told him so.

Jamie's shot fired like a cannonball straight into the corner of the net. And Leon Tibbs got nowhere near it. Even two Leon Tibbs' wouldn't have kept it out!

The strike had so much power it almost the burst right through the net.

Jamie couldn't believe it. He had actually scored a goal at Hawkstone United!

The crowd immediately went berserk. The fans were celebrating as if Hawkstone had just won the Cup!

Jamie was in a daze of ecstasy, but before he had the chance to celebrate, he saw Leon Tibbs racing out of his goal, heading straight for him...

Jamie started to jog towards the tunnel, with Tibbs's shouts ringing in his ears.

"Oi, titch! Where d'you think you're going?" the 'keeper bellowed. "You stay right where you are!"

It was certainly lucky for Jamie that, seemingly from nowhere, Harry Armstrong suddenly appeared, putting his body between Tibbs and Jamie.

Even Tibbs knew not to mess with Harry Armstrong.

"Jamie looks like he's going be some player, doesn't he, Leon?" smiled Harry calmly. "Get your composure back, 'Keeps. We're kicking off in a second."

But Tibbs was still seething with anger at having been beaten by an 11-year-old mascot.

"No one does that to me!" he snarled.

"Exactly..." agreed Harry Armstrong.

18

Remember The Name

As the two teams got ready to start the game, the stadium announcer's booming voice came on the tannoy.

"OK, before he goes, let's say a big thank you to our mascot for today, Jamie Johnson! And if what we've just seen is anything to go by, that is probably a name we should all remember!"

Jamie raised his hand, a little shyly.

He could not believe what had just happened. He had produced his best-ever piece of skill in front of 37,000 fans. It was almost as though being on this stage, playing on this pitch, had taken Jamie's talent to another level.

Then, slowly at first, from one pocket of supporters initially, but quickly spreading through the ground like a hungry fire, a chant got louder and louder until it seemed that every fan in the ground was on their feet singing the same words:

"One Jamie Johnson! There's only one Jamie Jooohhhnson. There's only ooone Jamieeee Johhhnson!"

Jamie's heart burned with pride. He loved the feeling of being cheered by so many people. He hoped they would never stop.

Confident now, he turned to wave to the crowd in every corner of the ground.

As the appreciation for him got louder and louder, Jamie smiled and leapt into the air, punching his fist skyward.

This was the first time that thousands of football fans stood up to sing Jamie's name and applaud his talent. But it wouldn't be the last. This boy was born to play…

EXTRA TIME

WELCOME TO YOUR SECRET BONUS CONTENT!

CHECK OUT WHAT'S COMING YOUR WAY...

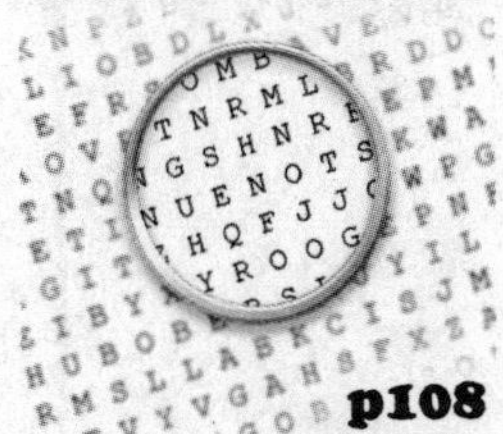

Mega-Hard JJ Wordsearch!

E	K	Q	O	V	U	P	T	E	Z	Q	B	G	T	C
N	E	Y	B	N	D	S	J	C	Z	O	C	O	O	B
E	L	K	N	P	Z	B	P	N	Y	K	C	C	O	L
K	K	L	I	O	B	D	L	X	J	S	P	S	O	N
C	C	E	F	R	S	O	M	B	A	V	E	V	E	O
I	A	O	V	R	T	N	R	M	L	B	R	D	D	C
K	T	N	Q	N	G	S	H	N	R	F	E	P	M	K
D	E	T	I	N	U	E	N	O	T	S	K	W	A	H
A	G	I	T	Z	H	Q	F	J	J	O	W	P	G	G
E	I	B	Y	X	Y	R	O	O	G	E	P	N	E	O
H	U	B	O	B	E	P	S	L	J	Y	I	L	G	A
R	M	S	L	L	A	B	K	C	I	S	J	M	A	L
E	T	V	Y	V	G	A	H	S	F	X	Z	A	A	Y
V	F	T	H	U	G	O	B	O	G	S	O	N	C	J
O	G	G	M	I	K	E	P	N	A	D	Q	L	B	K

Jamie found all these in 12 minutes! See if you can beat his time! Good luck!!

1. BORNTOPLAY
2. GOAL
3. HAWKSTONEUNITED
4. HUGOBOGSON
5. JACK
6. JAMIEJOHNSON
7. LEONTIBBS
8. MASCOT
9. MIKE
10. OVERHEADKICK
11. SICKBALL
12. STRIKE
13. TACKLE
14. TYLERFORBES

On The Spot!

KEY FOOTY QUESTIONS WITH DAN FREEDMAN

Who are your favourite footballers of all time?

It's difficult to look beyond Messi. The guy is simply incredible. When I interviewed him I really wanted to know what it felt like to be the greatest player on the planet! Also, Marco van Basten is an all-time hero. Check out his bicycle kick for Ajax v Den Bosch. Outstanding!

Do you get much fan mail from your readers?

Yes, with Twitter, my website, emails and letters, there are lots of ways for Jamie Johnson fans to get in touch with me and I always make sure I respond. Being an author, you tend to spend a fair bit of time writing on your own, so hearing from people who have read the books is always a brilliant moment. It makes all the hard work worth it!

What was it like writing about Jamie before he was famous?

It was great. At one stage, even the best footballers in the world – people like Messi and Ronaldo – were just football-mad schoolkids! So we can all empathize with Jamie's dream of making it to the top. Going back and writing a prequel was fun for me as an author too because I already know what happens to Jamie next...

What's it like having your books turned into a TV series?

It's been an amazing experience. Jamie Johnson has been a character in my head for so many years. Now, to see him brought to life on the screen is wonderful. I even got to have a kick around with 'Jamie' during filming, which was a great moment! While there are differences between the books and TV series, the spirit of the stories are very much the same.

What's your favourite thing about writing about Jamie Johnson and who is he based on?

I get to sit and daydream about football! That's my job! I also find Jamie very intriguing as a character. I always say that, with Jamie, you're never quite sure what he's going to do. Is he going to turn around, produce a sensational bit of skill and belt one in from 35 yards? Or is he going to lose his temper, do something he regrets and get himself sent off? Characters like that keep you guessing, which is great for the readers and the author. Jamie is partly based on me (we have a fair bit in common) and partly based on the great players I have been lucky enough to meet. People like Ronaldo, Messi, Rooney... I have taken a little bit from each of these players, added them to my own character and experiences ... and the result is Jamie Johnson. He is the kind of player I would love to see play live.

If you had to pick any footballer to have a kick around with, who would it be?
Good question. I've got massive respect for Steven Gerrard. He offered me his support before The Kick Off came out, when I was a completely unknown author, and I'll never forget that. Thierry Henry is a man full of charisma and intelligence. David Beckham and Gary Lineker are both legends as people, never mind what they have achieved in the game. Messi and Ronaldo have both taken football to a new level... But perhaps, at the moment, I would like to have a kick around with Gareth Bale. He's been a left winger – like Jamie – and there are lots of similarities between their stories too, so I have a whole load of questions I need to ask him!

What's the best game you've ever seen live?
I was lucky enough to watch the World Cup Quarter Final: Brazil v England in Japan in 2002 and then fly home on the plane to London with the England players afterwards. I'll never forget it...

Can you please answer one final question: are 'sickballs' actually real?

You bet they are! I was working with a school in East London and a teacher told me about the kids making them in the playground. The thought of it was so disgusting that I decided I had to include it in the book! So now everyone has that same mental image too!

If you have your own questions for Dan, visit his website

www.DanFreedman.co.uk

He answers every message he gets

Dan Freedman's Football Brain Teasers!

1. Which popstar was Lionel Messi named after?

2. Which Portuguese club did Cristiano Ronaldo leave to join Manchester United?

3. Which player's career went like this?

   Man United → Preston (loan) → Real Madrid → LA Galaxy → AC Milan (loan) → LA Galaxy → Paris St Germain (loan)

4. Wayne Rooney is England's record goalscorer. Which player did he take the record from?

5. At which club did Gareth Bale, Theo Walcott and Luke Shaw all begin their careers?

6. Which club has Jose Mourinho NOT managed? Porto, Chelsea, Inter Milan, Bayern Munich, Real Madrid, Manchester United

7. Pep Guardiola was a midfielder when he played. Did he ever play international football for Spain?

8. How many times have Brazil won the World Cup?

9. Dennis Bergkamp, Johan Cruyff and Zlatan Ibrahimovic have all played for which club?

10. What number shirt did both Pelé and Diego Maradona wear?

How do you think you did? Check your answers on the next page. No peeking if you haven't finished!!

Quiz answers

1. Lionel Richie
2. Sporting Lisbon
3. David Beckahm
4. Bobby Charlton
5. Southampton
6. Bayern Munich
7. Yes, he played 47 times for Spain, scoring 5 goals.
8. Five
9. Ajax
10. 10

Want more great football drama?

Follow Jamie's journey to the top
Collect the whole series!

Special prequel

Book 1

Book 2

Book 3

Book 4

Book 5

Book 6

Want more JJ action?

Here's your exclusive sneak peek at the start of...

DAN FREEDMAN

1

What Makes You So Special?

Tuesday 29 April

"Jamie Johnson!" Mr Pratley shouted, his hot, smelly coffee breath roaring like a dirty hurricane into Jamie's face.

He had grabbed Jamie's scribbled formation of a Hawkstone United team with all his favourite players and, of course, *J Johnson* as number 11, the left- winger.

This was far from the first time that Jamie had been caught playing fantasy football instead of listening. When it came to football, Jamie's brain was like a powerful computer, working out teams, angles, shots and passes ... but when it came to listening to Pratley, well, Jamie just seemed to switch off as soon as the man started talking. It drove Pratley wild with rage.

"Have you any idea how many boys have been through this school and claimed that they were going to be a footballer when they grew up? Hundreds ... thousands!"

Mr Pratley was now tearing up Jamie's sheet into as many little pieces as possible. The more he ripped the page into smaller and smaller sections, the redder his face became and the wider his eyes bulged.

Jamie did not respond. He couldn't. It was taking every ounce of his power not to burst into laughter. All he could do was stare at the big green bogey that was hovering, tantalizingly loose, from the end of Mr Pratley's nostril. It was a beauty: wet and sticky yet still hard enough to be absolutely ripe for the picking.

"And of those thousands of boys," Pratley continued, the redness now rising from his face into his big, shiny, balding head, "... who ALL thought they were going to be a professional football player ... who ALL thought they were

God's gift to the game – just like you no doubt do – have you any idea how many of them did it? How many of them became footballers?"

Jamie shook his head. He'd noticed that the more Pratley was getting worked up and the louder he shouted, the more the bogey had begun to wobble. It was as though it was dancing to the beat of Pratley's anger.

Pratley walked to the front of the classroom and chucked the remnants of Jamie's sheet into the bin. Then he turned and marched back towards Jamie.

The closer he got, the better the view Jamie had of the bogey. It was now doing something amazing. When Pratley breathed out, the bogey poked further out of his nose, as if it were waving to the world. And when he breathed in, it returned slightly further back up his nostril. It appeared to be on some kind of invisible string.

"None!!" barked Pratley. "Not one of those boys became professional footballers! So, I would like you to tell me why you think you are any different."

Jamie looked at his best friend, Jacqueline – or, Jack, as everyone knew her – for help. She shook her head. *Don't talk back*. That's what she was saying to him with her eyes. And she was right. This was a regular occurrence between Jamie and Mr Pratley. For some reason, Jamie had the ability to wind up Pratley more than any other kid in the whole school. The kids found it hysterical but right now, they had reached the danger zone; one more word from Jamie and Pratley might just explode.

Of course there were plenty of things Jamie could have said; lots of arguments he could have put forward to explain why he believed that, one day, he would become a professional footballer: that he was by far the best player in the school ... that he got all his talent from his granddad, who, had it not been for the injury, would easily have been one of Hawkstone's greatest- ever players ... that he trained and practised every single day because he wanted to become not *just* a professional footballer but one of the best players in the world...

But he didn't say anything. Jack was right. They both knew that whenever Jamie answered back, it only made Pratley even angrier. The best course of action Jamie could take now would be to say nothing. Nothing at all.

And so Jamie just shrugged his shoulders and stayed quiet.

"Answer me, Johnson!" yelled Pratley. "Or I'll keep you in here for the whole of lunchtime by yourself. What makes you think you're so special? What makes you think you've got something that all the other boys didn't?"

Pratley's face was now just an inch from Jamie's. The bogey was smack bang in front of Jamie's eyes. It was moving in and out of the teacher's nose, perfectly in time with Pratley's pants of fury.

Out of the corner of his eye, Jamie saw Jack turn away. Her body was chugging. She had seen it too and had started laughing without making any noise.

Jamie could feel it coming inside him too. It was rising up through his body like an unstoppable river from his lungs, into his throat and now it was at his mouth. The laughter could not be controlled for very much longer.

"For the very last time, Johnson! Why do you think you are better than any of them?"

"I don't know..." Jamie finally stuttered. The laughter was already leaking out. He knew he was going to get into trouble anyway, so he thought he might as well make it worth it. "*Snot* really for me to say!"

2

The Day of Destiny

"We'll know tomorrow!" shouted Jack, grabbing Jamie by his shirt and dragging him out of lunch.

"Know what?" he asked, laughing as she tugged him all the way to the Assembly Hall.

"TOMORROW!" she repeated, pushing him face to face with the sheet of paper that announced their day of destiny.

Teachers v Pupils

Football Match

The date for this game
has been confirmed!

All details will be
announced in assembly tomorrow

Jamie stared at the notice.

It concerned the football match that he had being looking forward to all year. The match between the teachers of Wheatlands School and the pupils of Year 6. The match that was going to be the biggest of Jamie's life.

Jamie and Jack gazed at the Wheatlands School Football Trophy. Gleaming like treasure, it stood, as always, in its special cabinet in the Assembly Hall. It remained there for the whole year until, on the day of the game itself, the head teacher, Mr Karenza, removed the prize from the cabinet and handed it to the winning captain to lift into the air.

Since they had joined the school, Jamie and Jack had been forced to watch, helpless from the sidelines, as the previous Year 6 pupils' teams had suffered embarrassing losses at the hands of the teachers.

But this year Jamie and Jack were in Year 6. Now it was their chance to play and put things right … to finally put one over on the teachers.

They had promised themselves that, in this game, things would be different ... that this would be *their* year.

However, just one look at the wooden board – upon which was engraved the results of all the previous matches – spelled out the difficulty of the task that lay ahead.

And it also named the teacher who would be standing in their way.

Teachers V Pupils
The Results

Teachers 11 – 8 Pupils	Winning Captain: C Pratley
Teachers 6 – 4 Pupils	Winning Captain: C Pratley
Teachers 4 – 4 Pupils	Match abandoned
Teachers 8 – 1 Pupils	Winning Captain: C Pratley
Teachers 7 – 3 Pupils	Winning Captain: C Pratley
Teachers 5 – 2 Pupils	Winning Captain: C Pratley
Teachers 9 – 6 Pupils	Winning Captain: C Pratley
Teachers 5 – 3 Pupils	Winning Captain: C Pratley
Teachers 7 – 6 Pupils	Winning Captain: C Pratley
Teachers 6 – 4 Pupils	Winning Captain: C Pratley
Teachers – Pupils	Winning Captain:

3
10,000 Hours

"Come on then," said Jack. "Spit it out."

She and Jamie were walking back home from school together, as they did every day, kicking an old drink can between them along the street.

Jamie shook his head. Sometimes, he didn't like to talk. Even to Jack.

"Look," she said. "You always tell me eventually, so why don't we just skip past the silent bit and get to the talking bit?"

Jamie stared at her. Jack constantly surprised and impressed him. It had been the same since the day he'd met her. They had played football and he had thought that, because she was a girl, she might not be that good. Instead she had proved to be one of the best goalkeepers he had ever seen! Since that day, they had been pretty much inseparable, and sometimes Jamie felt that Jack knew him better than he knew himself.

"It's that stuff Pratley was saying today," he began. "That I'm no different to all the other kids that wanted to be footballers and didn't make it... I know I was laughing and stuff, but I can't get it out of my head."

"You're not still worried about Pratley, are you?" she said. "Just because he's a teacher doesn't mean he knows everything. My dad always says that the people that make the rules aren't any better than the rest of us."

"Yeah," said Jamie. "But what if Pratley's actually right? What if I am no better than the others?"

"OK. So what are you going to do about it?" Jack responded immediately.

"What?" said Jamie. He was shocked by her abruptness and missed his kick of the can.

"Well, you can either keep worrying about it, thinking you're no better than everyone else, or you can start making it happen ... doing something to give yourself that extra edge."

Jamie smiled at her. Jack was the cleverest person he knew but he had no idea what she was going on about.

"How many hours did your granddad Mike say you'd have to practise if you wanted to become a professional footballer?" she asked.

"Ten thousand," said Jamie. It was one of the many pieces of advice Mike had given him about football. He'd said that the top players only looked so good because they had practised so long and from a very young age.

Ten thousand hours seemed a huge amount to reach but, for Jamie, every second playing football was pure joy.

"Cool," said Jack, flicking the can into the air. "So let's get to the park and get practising!"

And with that she volleyed the can all the way over to the other side of the street, where it looped perfectly into a nearby skip.

Jamie breathed a little more easily. He still felt hurt and worried by Pratley's comments but, at the same time, having Jack's support always gave him a lift.

Jamie was an electrifyingly quick left winger and Jack was a brave and athletic goalkeeper. Together they made a pretty good pair, which was lucky because they both knew that, if they were going to stand any chance of beating the teachers and claiming that gleaming trophy at the end of the year, they would need to be part of the best pupils' team in the history of Wheatlands School.

"A great story about the true magic of football!"
– Lúcio, Brazilian football legend

JAMIE JOHNSON

Skills from Brazil

Jamie Johnson's going to learn from the best

DAN FREEDMAN